The Gold Doubloon Mystery

A Captain Finn Treasure Mystery
Book 3

LIZ DODWELL

Liz Dodwell

The Gold Doubloon Mystery: A Captain Finn Treasure Mystery
Copyright © 2014 by Liz Dodwell
www.lizdodwell.com

www.mix-booksonline.com

Print ISBN-10: 1939860156
Print ISBN-13: 978-1-939860-15-6
Published by Mix Books, LLC

Table of Contents

Liz Dodwell

For Dominic,
who is seeking the treasure of his destiny

ONE

The first of the reef sculptures was ready to be lowered into the water. The cremated remains of a woman had been mixed with environmentally-safe concrete and formed into a huge starfish, which now hung over the side of the boat. We hadn't known the woman in life, nor did we know any of the people who had gathered to watch her take her place amongst the sea life. We were there to memorialize the life of Ned "Guppie" Zawacki, an old-time treasure-hunting friend and mentor of Finn's. Ned had died without family, and pretty much broke. In fact, Finn and I were about the only people there for him at the end, and it was Finn who had commissioned the bell-shaped tribute that would become part of the artificial reef. By the way, in case you're wondering about the Guppie moniker, it's because of the way Ned used to purse his lips when he was thinking hard.

Sea Spirit Reef is about three miles off the coast of Jupiter in Florida. It was loosely modeled after Port Royal, Jamaica, which sank into the ocean back in the late 1600s after a massive earthquake. You might think the theme a bit off-key as a memorial, Port Royal having been notorious for pirates, prostitutes and booze and all. But there are nearly 2,000 of these reefs throughout the country, so having just one for those of us who like things a little quirky is OK in my book.

So, back to the story. We were respectfully waiting our turn to send Ned into the sea that he loved, along with about a dozen other small groups. A couple of divers were in the water, ready to guide the concrete starfish to its final destination. The rope around the sculpture had been crackling with the tension of its weight when, suddenly, it snapped. The starfish plunged into the water, narrowly missing one of the divers. A couple of women screamed, while most of us were momentarily immobilized in surprise.

Finn was the first to recover, rushing to the side to make sure the divers were OK. The rest of us streamed after him and peered into the depths. Two distinct sets of bubbles rose where the two divers were no doubt working to set the sculpture in place. "What's that?" someone said, pointing to another slight disturbance on the surface; nothing much, just a circular rippling really. Then something broke through the ripples and settled gently into the rhythm of the sea.

"Is that a fish?" an uncertain voice asked.

We all strained forward a little more to see better. This time, a lot of people screamed, as they realized it was no fish. It was a body.

TWO

For the past couple of weeks we'd been staying at the home of Russ and Viviana Kearns in Fort Pierce, which is just a little north of Jupiter. Russ had been curator at a privately run shipwreck museum in the Florida Keys. Over the years, Finn contributed a number of artifacts to the museum and got to know Russ pretty well. When Russ retired a year ago, he and Viviana left the Keys to be closer to their family. Actually, Russ would have preferred to stay where they were, but the trade-off was that Viviana OK'd the purchase of a boat for treasure hunting. So Russ found himself a great deal; a 1973 42-foot Cris Craft Commander Sports Fisherman for $25,000. He put another $20,000 into it, including a 24-inch mailbox – that's a blower mounted on the stern that excavates holes in the ocean sediment – and had himself a really sweet treasure boat.

The Kearns had an apartment over the garage and they'd been kind enough to let Finn and me stay there while planning Guppie's memorial. Our real home is Finn's 48-foot re-fitted aluminum crew boat, *Time Voyager*. We have a permanent berth at Mud Bug, a private island off the west coast of Florida. And let me explain, Finn is my mentor, a father figure to me. When things were really bad for me a few years ago, he gave me a chance and got me back on the right path. Ever since then I've had the good fortune to share his life and his work.

Finn's name is actually Rex Finsmer, though everyone calls him Finn, or Captain Finn. He's been a full-time shipwreck treasure hunter for at least three decades, and is the most amazing person I know. One of my jobs is to book speaking tours for him and I never tire of listening to his stories of shipwrecks, lost treasure or the Spanish Main. Oh, and I'm Phillida Jane Trent, but you can call me Phill.

As I was saying, we'd been at the Kearn's home for a while and, weather and time permitting, had gone out with Russ searching for artifacts and coin from the 1715 Spanish Plate Fleet. For those of you who don't know, the Fleet was actually a combined armada of 11 ships. Laden with gold, silver, jewels and treasures of the Orient, they departed Havana, Cuba for the voyage back to Spain. As they followed the east coast of Florida they were struck by a ferocious hurricane. Ten of the galleons were lost, as well as more than a thousand souls. The thing that always amazes me the most, though, is that 1500 survived.

So far, we'd found bones, iron spikes, pottery sherds and a coral-encrusted dead-eye that was definitely very old. It was the dead-eye that excited Finn the most; he said it's the best clue that we were in the right area.

Anyway, after the memorial fiasco the previous day, Finn thought it best we hang around on dry land for a couple of days. The Coast Guard had closed off the Sea Spirit Reef area pending investigation of a potential crime scene, which meant that Guppie's service was on hold. We had no idea if the corpse was a murder victim or an accidental death. We were able see it was a man, fully clothed. Obviously, he hadn't drowned taking an afternoon swim, but he might have fallen from a boat, maybe one of the cruise ships in and out of the eastern Florida ports.

As it turned out, it was a good thing we didn't go treasure hunting. About mid-morning, Finn got a call from the Palm Beach County constabulary, very nicely asking if he could help them with their inquiries. It was more than an hour's drive from the Kearns' home to the Sheriff's office, assuming the traffic was light, which of course it pretty much never is, so Finn settled on a one o' clock meeting.

"Is everyone being called in?" I asked.

"You weren't."

"Hmm. Good point. Then they must need your expertise for something."

A successful treasure hunter needs pretty good powers of deductive reasoning. Finn was one of the best, and he'd put those skills to use a few times helping solve crimes in the past. I wondered what the police thought he could do for them now.

We arrived at the police station about 15 minutes ahead of time. I say, "we," though technically I hadn't been invited, but I could be really stubborn when I wanted something, and I wanted to know what was going on. The first clue that this was more than an accidental drowning was when we were told we were to see Detective Lisandro Batista of the Homicide Unit. We were shown into a spartan interview room with the obligatory table and four chairs, and told the detective would be with us shortly.

"Well, at least we haven't been chained to the desk."

Finn just rolled his eyes at my lame joke. Truth to tell, I was a little uncomfortable. The atmosphere reminded me of too many places I'd been in when I was getting shuffled round the foster care system as a kid.

The door opened and Adam Rodriguez walked in. Well, not really, but this guy was practically a ringer for the hunky actor. If you know me, you know I'm not the type of woman who worries about her hair or the clothes she wears, but damn, I wished I'd paid attention to my appearance that day. The best I could do was suck my stomach in and thrust my chest out, 'cause it was the primary asset I had.

"Detective Lisandro Batista. Thank you for coming in." He held out his hand to Finn. "And you need no introduction, Captain Finn. I've followed your adventures for some years. It's an honor to meet you."

They shook briefly, then Batista turned to me, hand out and eyes raised in question. Oh, my god, those eyes were like deep rich carnelians.

"She's Phillida Trent," Finn coughed discreetly.

"What? Oh...right. That's me, um, call me Phill." *Good lord, I sounded like a blithering idiot.* I grabbed Batista's hand and shook with way too much gusto, and felt pathetically grateful when he didn't show the slightest reaction to my awkwardness. Woman probably swooned over him all the time, anyway.

Without a word, he then pulled something from his pocket and set it on the table in front of Finn. When he lifted his hand away, a gold coin was revealed.

"What can you tell me about this?"

Finn weighed it in his hand. "It's certainly gold." He keeps a small jeweler's loupe on his keychain – a loupe is a magnifier for up-close viewing – with which he scrutinized the coin.

"It's a 1714 J, Philip V, Mexico Mint 8 escudo cob."

"Can you explain that?"

"The capital 'M' with the small 'o' to the left of the shield tells us this is from the Mexico mint. The 'J' is the assayer's mark. You can clearly see the date, which was during the reign of Philip V of Spain; and the roman numerals, 'VIII,' refer to the coin's denomination. It appears to have some sand-washing, so I'd say it's a shipwreck coin, but in remarkably good condition."

"What is a 'cob' coin?"

"It's the gold doubloon of pirate treasure stories. The coins were struck by hand and very carefully weighed by the assayer, who snipped any excess gold from the edges. That's why no two are the same shape."

"And the Mexico Mint?"

"The Spanish had a dozen mints throughout the New World, but only a few of them struck gold coins – Mexico, Lima, Bogota and Cuzco."

Batista looked thoughtful as he digested the information. "Is there anything else you can tell me about this particular coin? Anything unusual, perhaps?"

"I'm afraid not. Though I wouldn't be at all surprised if it came from the 1715 Fleet."

"And what would its value be?"

Finn paused for a few moments. "I would say up to $8,000."

Batista rose. "Thank you, Captain. This has been most educational."

Whoa! We were being dismissed when we hadn't learned anything new. I raised my eyebrows at Finn but he was already on his feet.

"You're welcome, detective. I'm glad to help any time, though it's always good to know what I'm helping with."

"Ah." Batista tapped his finger to his lips. "As I'm sure you know, Captain, I am not at liberty to divulge details of an ongoing investigation," I snorted loudly; Batista chose to ignore me, "but I see no harm in giving you the dead man's identification. It will be public knowledge by tomorrow, anyway. He is Rick Marchand, owner of a small and moderately successful insurance agency, who has a loving wife and two nice teenage kids."

"How long had he been under?"

"I'm still awaiting the coroner's report, but we're guessing just a couple of days."

"Did he drown?"

"Aaah. No." Batista hesitated a moment, then continued. "He was shot in the back of the head."

"And the coin?"

The detective shook his head. "Sorry. You understand." He then escorted us back to the entrance where we said our goodbyes. As we reached the sidewalk we heard a shout, "Captain! Wait!" and Batista strode to us.

"Look, I could use some help with this case so I'm going to go out on a limb here, but I need your assurance this will go no further." He looked pointedly at me. *Of all the nerve.*

"You've got it," Finn said.

"The gold cob had been shoved into Marchand's throat. I figure it's a message of some sort, but I don't know what. Does that have any meaning to you?"

"Nothing I can think of right now. I'll look into it, though." Batista gave a look of some alarm and Finn raised his hand, "Discreetly, of course."

"Much appreciated. Here's my card; my cell number is on it. Call any time."

This time when we said our goodbyes, that was the end of it.

Liz Dodwell

THREE

"OK, now you can tell me. What's the significance of the coin?"

"I've no idea."

We were driving back to the Kearn's home, and I expected Finn to have solved the puzzle already, so I was taken aback at his response.

"Come on! Do the numbers add up to anything? Is there anything special about the year 1714? Maybe our attention is being directed to a shipwreck. Oh, maybe someone found another big treasure trove, like the Atocha." I was getting excited now. Nuestra Senora de Atocha held a 450 million dollar cache of silver, gold, emeralds and artifacts. The Spanish galleon was discovered by Mel Fisher, and is the dream of treasure hunters everywhere. "Seriously, Finn, this could be big."

"Maybe, maybe not."

I ground my teeth. I hated when Finn was in one of his contrary moods.

"What if there's some secret society, or even a serial killer and this is his trademark?"

"That's a pretty expensive trademark."

"Well, it must mean something!"

"I expect it must."

"You know, you can be so aggravating... I need a drink."

When we got back, Russ was outside with another, younger, guy. There was a definite family resemblance, so I was guessing this was his son. Sure enough, he introduced him as Russell, Jr.

"To avoid confusion, though, he goes by RJ."

RJ was the kind of guy who should be in a health club commercial. Not an ounce of body fat on him and a tan that said he spent a lot of time outdoors. I asked what he did for a living.

"I'm a private trainer."

"My son has a pretty nice life up in St. Augustine," Russ added. "He's able to set his own schedule and make time to go treasure diving in between." *Bingo.*

"Had any success?" Finn asked.

Russ butted in. "Why don't we head inside. Viv is fixing one of her Colombian specialties; chicken empanadas. She fries them rather than baking them, and we can talk over a cold beer."

"Works for me," said Finn, "and we swung by the liquor store so Phill can create one of her specialty cocktails."

"Well, *that* will work for me," R. J. smiled.

He had a pretty sexy smile, I noticed... and a wedding ring.

The sun was disappearing with the promise of another beautiful day to come. We were all sated with Viviana's feast, and my version of a stinger cocktail had received accolades. I called it, "Shiver me Stinger," and simply made a frozen drink with the brandy and white crème de menthe, then added a splash of white rum on top.

Now we were relaxing on the porch with coffee. I don't usually like coffee after dinner but figured Viviana was fixing some special Colombian variety she'd grown up with. When I asked her about it she laughed. Said that she only started drinking coffee after coming to America because the stuff they drank in her home country was like dishwater. The quality coffee beans were all exported, the bad beans left for local consumption.

The guys were talking about treasure, of course. I realized Finn had managed to bring the subject around to gold coins. *The sly fox.*

"There's a rumor going around that someone found a fleet coin recently; an 8 escudo."

"Not that I've heard," RJ said. "From which site?"

Known 1715 Fleet shipwreck site locations are given names such as "Cabin Wreck," "Corrigan's Wreck," and "Colored Beach Wreck." To work within three miles of the coast a permit is required from the state. It's easy to buy a research permit but exploration and recovery permits can get expensive, if you can get one at all. The idea behind this is that shipwrecks won't be wantonly destroyed. Sounds good, but it becomes too expensive for professional salvors to work these sites, so less honorable ones just take what they can get away with. Meanwhile, treasures that could be saved for posterity are simply left to be buried deeper into the sand, never to be seen or appreciated.

Anyway, this is why every now and then an object will appear on the black market, and Finn was "feeling out" Russ and RJ to see if they knew anything about the coin.

"Where did you hear that?" Russ asked.

"You know how it is, Russ. The treasure-hunting community is pretty small and word spreads faster than a slippery sailfish. Supposedly, it was a Mexico Mint cob."

At that moment, Viviana stood. "If you guys are going to talk business, I have work to do in the kitchen."

"I'll give you a hand."

"Thanks, Phill, but I can manage."

I insisted, and picked up the dirty glasses and followed her into the house. There wasn't a lot of cleaning up but I like to do my part, so I dried and polished the glassware and made idle chitchat as Viviana washed.

There was a small photo on a shelf above the sink: a younger Russ and Viviana with two small children, a boy and a girl.

"Oh, you have a daughter," I said. "Is she also in Florida?"

Viviana hesitated. "She is in Miami."

"That must work well. You're not far from either of your kids. You must get to see a lot of them."

There was no reply, and I was astonished and disconcerted when I looked at Viviana and saw tears seeping from her eyes.

"Are you OK? Did I say something?"

She bit her lip. "No. No, I… Irina is not well. I find it hard to talk…."

"I'm so sorry, I didn't mean…"

Viviana grabbed my arm. "It's fine. I'll be fine. You go back and join the guys. I just need a few minutes."

Lamely I mumbled more apologies and backed away. I suck at emotional scenes and the coward in me was more than thankful to do as asked. Quietly, I inserted myself back into the conversation on the porch, but the evening was winding down and soon Finn and I said our goodnights and went to the little apartment. We didn't see Viviana again.

"Did you learn anything?" I asked.

"Russ and I had a general chat about 1715 fleet coins. He said he hasn't come across anything since he was at the museum. They had a couple of gold cobs on display but he seems to think I know more about this than he does anyway."

"He's right about that, I'm sure. There's hardly anyone who knows more than you do." People came to Finn all the time for his opinion on shipwreck coins and treasure. He'd even been a featured expert on TV a couple of times. Heck, I was living with a celebrity… sort of.

"I put my foot in it a bit with Viviana."

"What do you mean?"

"I asked about their daughter and she started crying, said she was ill. Do you know anything about it?"

"Actually, I do." Finn looked thoughtful. "The girl has Down syndrome."

"Oh, how sad."

"Not necessarily. She was a lovely and well-loved child who became a relatively high-functioning adult. She had a job and her own apartment. Russ was really proud of her but, now that I think about it, he hasn't mentioned her in a long time."

"Perhaps something has happened. How old is she?"

"Mid-20s, I should say. A lot younger than RJ. She was an unexpected, though happy, surprise."

"Well, this day has been a bit of a downer. I managed to upset our host and we're getting nowhere with the gold doubloon. It's time I headed to bed. See you in the morning."

The only reply I got was a grunt and the click of the TV turning on. Finn would spend half the night lying awake and mulling over things with the television droning in the background. He did some of his best brainstorming that way. Seriously, I didn't think it was worth it. We had no personal interest in the case, unless old Guppie was in touch with Finn from the grave. And nobody was paying for our services. Finn would never let it go, though. That gold coin could be a clue to a wealth of treasure, and when it came to treasure, Finn was a sea dog with a bone.

Liz Dodwell

FOUR

When I got up the next morning I found Finn asleep on the couch. Our little apartment had a small kitchenette, so I stumbled that way and put the coffee on. When it was done I poured a cup, black and strong, and set it on the little table beside Finn then headed for the bathroom.

After I'd showered and dressed I found the coffee's aroma had done its trick. A bleary-eyed Finn was awake. I grabbed myself a cup of coffee. "What's on the agenda for the day?"

"Where's that card Batista gave us? I'd like to get down on the reef site, take a look around."

"You think you're likely to find anything of help?"

"Probably not, but we shouldn't leave any urn unturned, as they say."

"Finn, why are we doing this? We could be out working the fleet site and maybe find something and make some money. Instead, we're investigating a crime that's nothing to do with us."

Finn gave me a hard look. "If nothing else we owe it to Guppie. He deserves better than to have his memorial screwed up."

"Actually, I think Guppie would have got a kick out of it."

"That's true, but he would also chase that gold coin until he found it. And let's not forget, a man has been murdered. That's not something I can easily walk away from."

I sighed. Like I said, a sea dog with a bone.

Later that morning we met Batista down at the dock in Palm Beach. He been more than happy for Finn to take a look at the reef site, and had arranged a police boat to take us out there. I was surprised when he got in the boat with us.

"You going to dive?"

"I'm not going to miss an opportunity to learn something from an old master like Finn."

Okay then. I'd been undecided about diving. Underwater is not my natural element but I didn't want to seem like chicken shit in front of my dream man, and I was kind of curious about the memorial reef itself. So about an hour later I stripped to my swimsuit, wondering if Batista was noticing that I was actually in pretty good shape. Finn, as usual, was in shorts and a T-shirt. We'd brought our own gear, and when the three of us were ready, over the side we went, leaving two county cops in charge of the boat.

Swimming around the replica pillars and buildings was quite surreal. I could totally imagine Port Royal as it must've been in its pirate heyday. There was even a tavern with a whiskey bottle memorial laying inside. The plaque on the bottle read "Whiskey, a very special dog." *Cute.*

I'd been engrossed in my meanderings but now looked up to see where Finn and Batista had got to. Out of the blue something shot past me, hitting my arm as it went by then bouncing off one of the pillars. I was so startled my brain didn't register anything 'til a sudden burning pain brought my attention back to my arm. There was blood - my blood. Instinctively I opened my mouth and screamed. The mouthpiece fell out and I panicked. Before I knew it I was swallowing water, lots of water and beginning to feel dizzy. Something was coming towards me fast. *Oh God.* It was a shark - in a white T-shirt. It got hold of me; I thrashed around frantically, and that was the last thing I knew.

Liz Dodwell

FIVE

Waking up in a hospital bed is like an uncertain dream. It took a minute before the fog cleared and I realized where I was and what had happened. In a chair by the window Finn was sitting, head on chest, softly snoring.

"Finn." Nothing.

I tried a little louder. "Finn."

His head jerked up. "Hi, honey. How are you feeling?" And he came to the side of the bed.

"Okay, I guess. How long have I been here?"

"Just overnight. Your wound is not too bad but you swallowed a lot of water. Do you remember any of it?"

"Yeah. I was attacked by a shark wearing a white T-shirt."

Finn's eyes rolled skyward. "That shark was me, and you were fighting like hell while I was trying to save you."

"Oh. Thanks," I said softly.

"It's our detective friend you should be thanking. He got you to the surface a lot faster than I ever could and immediately started rapid breathing. And you were lucky we had a fast boat and oxygen. We came straight into Jupiter, an ambulance was waiting at the dock and brought you to the medical center."

"Batista gave me the kiss of life?" Finn looked heavenward. "My dream man kissed me and I didn't even know it. Life can be so unfair."

"Do you want to know what happened or not?"

"Sorry. Go on."

"You were shot with a harpoon. It sliced through some muscle in your upper arm; it's gonna hurt like a bitch for a few days but is certainly nothing life-threatening. Batista saw the shooter from a distance- a big man, broad and muscular - but he took off with a small underwater scooter so there was no way to catch him. And I guess the detective figured your need was greater anyway."

"Huh! So I was nearly killed for nothing."

"I wouldn't exactly say nothing, and I wouldn't say you were nearly killed. That was a warning."

I snorted, but decided to let the subject drop there.

"Where did the flowers come from?"

"That giant arrangement is from Russ and Viviana. The small one is from your detective."

"Batista sent me flowers? What a sweetheart." I smiled happily. "By the way, when am I getting out of here?"

"As soon as the doctor clears you this afternoon, then we're going to the marina where Rick Marchand kept his boat. Apparently, that's where he was killed."

"Is Batista meeting us there?"

Finn gave me one of those "enough already" looks.

"Alrighty then," I said.

The boat was on Dock B; a pretty new 25 foot Stingray cabin cruiser – nice. It was still taped off as a crime scene but Batista had sent word to the cop on guard that it was okay to let us on. Obviously he wasn't planning to show up himself. *Bummer.* We poked around for a while but other than a little blood there really was nothing to see.

"Another dead-end," I said. "Maybe it's time to head home. I miss Shrimp." Shrimp is our boat cat, a cute little calico that we rescued. She got her name because that's the only thing she'll respond to, shrimp being her favorite food and all.

"Sit down," Finn said. "Let's go over a few things."

We plopped down inside the boat where the cop wouldn't hear us and I waited for Finn to start.

"Okay, we have a gold doubloon but we can't be sure it's a fleet coin. We have the body of an ordinary, hard-working guy, who got his head blown in and the coin shoved down his throat. According to Batista there are no signs of a fight, so it seems he was taken unawares. He was then shoved overboard – there's a little blood on the gunwale – either dropped into a small boat or into the water, and then taken out to the reef memorial site. There the body was dumped and tied down. It wouldn't have taken any strength to kill him, but it would've required some effort to get him out to the reef."

"Somebody must not have done a good job of tying the corpse if it floated after only a couple of days."

"Only one leg was tied. The knot was professional but it looks like the killer was interrupted. Could have been anything from a shark to nearby fishermen. At any rate, this tells us the killer either knows the waters or knows how to navigate. We also know he's a diver and a big man, and he knows how to use a fishing harpoon. Now here is where I start to speculate.

"Forget the gold coin for now. The only person who knew we were going to the reef site with Batista was Russ. I checked with the detective and he assured me he didn't mention our names to anyone."

"I don't like where this is going."

"Neither do I, Phill. Russ could easily have told his wife and son where we were going. RJ is a big guy with diving and boating skills, and I'm pretty sure he knows how to use a harpoon."

"What earthly reason could RJ have for killing an insurance agent?"

"That's what we have to look into. Maybe they knew each other. RJ would know about cob coins. He might even have found one. I can think of a lot of possible scenarios, but we need the truth."

I drew a deep breath and let it out slowly. "So what do we do now?"

"Find out more about the Kearns family."

"You want me to do some digging?"

"No. Someone is willing to go to some pretty dangerous lengths to keep this thing quiet. I'm going to contact Sonny to see if he can trace where the gold doubloon came from, and have Bert research the Kearns. You and I are going to act like we've given up."

"You're not going to start treasure hunting again with Russ are you? I'm not at all comfortable about us being out in the wide waters with a potential killer."

"Don't worry. We'll say we're staying a couple more days to rearrange Guppie's memorial and then we'll be going back to Mud Bug. That should give the killer some breathing room."

I should explain, "Sonny" Scrivens is an international coin dealer. He's been "Sonny" for more than 70 years. You'd think he might have dropped the juvenile nickname by now in favor of his real name, but I'm not sure he knows what it is any more. Certainly, no-one else does. Anyway, he's semi-retired these days. He and Finn go back a long way and Sonny specializes in Spanish coins. Though his business has always been pretty legit, you can't be in the coin community for 60 years without developing contacts in all directions, if you know what I mean. So, if anyone can track the doubloon back, it's Sonny.

Bert is Elbert Lex Van Nifterik, multimillionaire, owner of Mud Bug Island and computer genius. We helped him out not so long ago, and in return he allows us free berth at his island paradise. And, while I know my way around a computer, I'm a complete bonehead compared to Bert.

While Finn made his calls, I poked around the Stingray. She was probably $70,000 to $80,000 of boat by my reckoning. I wondered if the insurance business was really that good.

"We're done here." Finn brought me out of my reveries. "Let's pick up some grub and take it back to the apartment. You don't look so good right now."

"I'm fine." I was lying: my arm hurt like hell and I was dead tired. In truth, I was ready to pop a couple of pain pills and crash. So we picked up egg rolls and ants climbing trees – one of my favorite spicy pork dishes over bean thread noodles – and later, I was the one who fell asleep on the couch.

SIX

Between the pills, and perhaps delayed shock, I slept really late. It was nearly 10 when I woke. Finn had thrown a blanket over me, my head was throbbing and someone had pulled woolly socks over my teeth in the night. At least, that's sort of what it felt like. I needed water. Actually, I needed water and more pain pills.

Finn was nowhere in sight, and I felt too lousy to really care, so I staggered into the shower and thanked God and the Kearns for hot water and a massaging showerhead. Of course, I'd forgotten I was supposed to keep the dressing on my arm dry. *Crap.*

I was trying to find something dry to cover my wound when Finn came back carrying chocolate croissants and fruit salad. That man knows me well. You could paint me pink and put me in a pig pen if you dangled chocolate croissant in front of me. Uh oh. Was Finn buttering me up for something? You never quite knew with him.

Turns out he was just being nice.

"I got your favorite," he said, "and there's coffee made."

"Already had some." I was busy stuffing my face with food.

"Well, when you're done with that, we got some information back from Bert. I left it open on the laptop; you should read it."

After I'd devoured three croissants I ate a little fruit, just to keep my diet balanced, you know, then read through Bert's notes about the Kearns. Bert had uncovered a missing person's report about their daughter, Irina. She'd been found within a day, but there was no detail about what happened or where she was. He'd also found a birth certificate for a child by Irina. No father was listed.

"So Irina went missing then had a baby. I get why Viviana doesn't like to talk about it but it has nothing to do with Marchand or the gold doubloon. Unless Marchand abducted her and I can think of no earthly reason why he'd do that. I don't see that this moves us any further forward."

"I'm not sure it does, either."

I could tell Finn was frustrated. The clues we had seemed to be all over the map, with nothing to join them. He was probably feeling cooped up, too. He just wasn't an indoor type of guy.

"Let's get out of here. You'll think better in the open air."

"Good idea. We can drive down to the marina again, where Marchand's boat is; ask around in case anybody saw anything."

"Haven't the police already done that?"

"Sure, but you never know."

Finn decided to take Route A1A along the coast to the Palm Beach area. It would take us twice as long but it was a really pretty drive down through Hobe Sound and Juno Beach, and we were in no hurry. It was one of those days we live for in Florida. An unseen hand had painted hazy streaks of white across a blue sky, then colored the tropical landscape an impossible green, and textured the water as if particles of light were suspended in it. We put down the top on our old yellow Saab and enjoyed the moment.

"You know, even if we could afford a Cadillac I think I'd keep Old Yeller." I patted her dashboard affectionately. She was a 1998 Saab 900 S that Finn had found for $500. At that time, she had been a dingy green with a fair bit of rust and a few other problems. We'd taken her to our buddy, Jafet Quintana, in Sarasota. He dives with us when we're over that way and is brilliant with anything mechanical. It just so happened that he had some yellow auto paint and the price was right – free. Hence, Old Yeller. And she was proving to be a faithful friend.

Two carefree hours after leaving Fort Pierce we arrived at the marina and parked. We headed for Dock B. The yellow crime scene tape was still on it but there was no police guard. Finn stared hard at the boat while I let my gaze wander 'til my eyes were riveted on something on the next dock over.

"Finn! Finn!" I shook his arm urgently and pointed across the water. "Look over there."

He followed the direction of my arm. "I'll be damned."

Sitting in the corresponding slip was another Stingray. She was white with the same dark blue stripe and dark blue Bimini top. She was a twin to the one we were standing next to. We looked at each other.

"This could change everything," Finn said. "We need to find the dockmaster."

Together we headed to the marina office. The door jangled as we stepped inside. A woman was behind the reception desk with her back to us. She was a little on the heavy side but in a voluptuous kind of way. When she turned she didn't disappoint from the front view either, and I saw Finn's eyes flicker open a little wider. He just can't help himself around a pretty woman. This one wasn't wearing a trace of makeup, nor did she need it with the warm skin color and healthy glow of someone who works in the sun.

"Can I help you?"

"We'd like to see the dockmaster," Finn said.

"Yes. How can I help you?"

For once, Finn was a little taken aback, but he recovered well, introducing himself and explaining our purpose in being there.

"I'm Moema Nuallain. Detective Batista had told me you would be here the other day but he did not say anything about today. You are asking for information on one of our clients and it is not our policy to give it out indiscriminately."

Oh great, she was going to be bitchy about this.

Finn smiled. "You're absolutely right to be cautious, Miss Nuallain. Why don't we save ourselves any difficulty and give Batista a call? Frankly, he needs to know about this, too."

"Please, call me Moe." She smiled back, tucking a length of slightly graying hair behind her ear. "If you would call, I'll fetch the record book."

"I think she likes me," Finn said in a low voice as he pulled out his phone.

Liz Dodwell

SEVEN

Batista was excited. I could hear it in his voice over the speakerphone as he talked to Finn. We were back at the apartment and the detective had run a check on the owner of the second Stingray. As he spoke, I took notes.

The boat was pretty much a carbon copy of Marchand's and belonged to Hemming Mathiasen, a Danish-born naturalized American, more usually known as Hammer. "To law enforcement," Batista explained, "he is known as a dealer in jewelry, gold and silver of uncertain origin." He went on to tell us that Hammer was based in New York City and had a rap sheet several yards long. "He started out as a low-class hoodlum, running drugs for the big guys and doing a little petty theft on the side. He dropped off the radar for a while. When he resurfaced, it seemed that somewhere along the way he hit it rich. Not really rich but enough that he could buy his way out of a lot of trouble and pay others to do his dirty work. At heart he's still just a low-class hoodlum and he's nasty, really nasty."

"Does Hammer look anything like Marchand?"

"You're thinking the same thing I am. This could be a case of mistaken identity."

"Well," Finn said, "Marchand's boat was in slip B-11; Hammer's was in C-11. The same location on parallel docks."

"We're looking into it."

After that Batista clammed up, using the ongoing investigation excuse, but he did add, "Tell Phill she did good to notice the other Stingray."

"You just did," said Finn.

As it happened, we'd learned a little more from Moe. It had cost Finn a future dinner, but he wasn't complaining. She had told us that Hammer had rented the slip four months previously and had been down at regular two week intervals since then. When he came down it was usually with an entourage. Thugs, she'd called them. Finn had asked if they all stayed on the boat. "Only Mathiasen," she'd replied.

Finn had also asked about any similarity of appearance. Moe had said Marchand and Mathiasen were similar build but completely different features, though both were fair-haired. "And Rick Marchand was a good guy. I wouldn't want to touch Mathiasen with a hundred foot barge pole."

"So," I was thinking aloud, "the killer can't have known Hammer, or he'd know he had the wrong man."

"He could have come up behind him without seeing his face and realized his mistake when it was too late. Either way, he still had to get rid of a body."

"But why get rid of the body at all? It's not like the killer really bought himself any time. And if that was his intent, he didn't have to cart the body all the way to the Sea Spirit Reef. He could have simply weighted it and dumped it almost anywhere."

"Maybe he just wanted to confuse things by making people wonder if the reef had any significance in the crime. We may never know."

At that moment, Finn's phone rang. "Sonny! What do you have for me?"

He gave an occasional grunt as he listened and his face drained of emotion. "Thanks, Sonny. I appreciate the help."

"Well?" I raised my eyebrows.

"I have to do some thinking."

"You have an idea what's going on, haven't you?"

"Pretty sure. And it's not good; not good at all. I need to do some serious thinking and be sure I'm not making a big mistake."

I knew I wouldn't get anything else out of him until he was ready, so I figured I may as well just go to bed.

Liz Dodwell

EIGHT

At ten o' clock sharp, the moment the store opened, we walked into *Everything Goes Pawn.* "Everything," seemed rather optimistic for what was, in fact, a very modestly-sized establishment. The clerk didn't seem too surprised to see us hanging by the door, though; simply gave a half-smile and said an unfeeling "Good morning."

Finn had been in touch with Bert again during the night and set him the task of discovering Irina's employer at the time she went missing. I'd been pumping Finn for information since I got up but he wasn't saying anything.

As we entered Finn immediately asked for Mr. Guzman. Bert, of course, had supplied information on the store owner. The clerk was hesitant but Finn insisted, telling him it was extremely urgent.

"Wait here," the fellow said.

Moments later an elderly man appeared from what must be a back office. He was dressed in a three-piece striped suit that was a little large for his slight, stooped frame. Heavy rimmed glasses hid much of his thin face but the eyes behind them seemed kind. He held out his hand.

"I'm Ezra Guzman, but you have the advantage of me."

We introduced ourselves and Finn asked if we could speak privately.

43

"What's this about?"

"I'm working with the Palm Beach police in a consultancy capacity," *that was stretching it a bit,* "on a case that might have something to do with Irina Kearns."

Guzman registered surprise. "You'd better come back." And he led us to an office barely bigger than a closet. We plopped on a couple of cheap plastic chairs and Guzman waited for us to begin.

We were with the man for an hour or so, and what he revealed in that time was both shocking and disgusting. It was obvious he'd been fond of Irina. "If you can do anything to help find these people," he'd said, "you have my full support."

As we walked out I glanced at Finn. *Oh, yeah.* He was in Lone Ranger mode alright.

NINE

We were in the Kearn's living room with Russ and Viviana. They were seated close together on the couch. The morning sun that flooded the room did nothing to brighten Viviana's pallid complexion, and her skin looked dry and papery. She clung to her husband's arm as if it were a lifeline, even though he slumped beside her with no more vigor than a limp pickle.

I had parked myself where I could observe without being too close, while Finn stood, looking grim, with one hand resting on the mantelpiece. For a fleeting moment I was reminded of Nemesis, the personification of indignation toward those who had committed crimes with apparent impunity. Was Finn going to be a "dispenser of dues" to Russ and Viviana? We all looked expectantly at him.

"From the beginning, we all thought this murder was about money and treasure. Why else the gold doubloon lodged in the dead man's throat? Had Rick Marchand found a treasure trove from the 1715 Fleet and cheated his partners? Had he stolen treasure from another diver? The coin, after all, appeared to be a shipwreck gold piece and, in fact, it was."

Here, Finn paused and put his finger to his mouth in momentary thought.

"We'll come back to the coin a little later. First, let me put before you all the known facts.

"A man is killed by a bullet to the back of the head. He is Rick Marchand, a local man, owner of a successful insurance agency, with a loving wife and family, and by all accounts a pillar of the community. He has no criminal record, not even a parking ticket. He owns a 25 foot Stingray cabin cruiser, white with a dark blue stripe and dark blue bimini top. This boat, which is called *Made My Bed*, he keeps at Dockyard Marina in slip number 11 on Dock B. It is on the boat that he is killed with a shot to the back of the head. A professional hit, according to the police. The body is then taken to the Sea Spirit Memorial Reef where the killer does a poor job of tying it down. Two days later, as a service is in progress on a boat above the reef, one of the concrete memorial stones breaks from its harness and falls to the reef, dislodging the corpse below."

A low moan escaped Viviana's lips. She was biting on her knuckles with her head down and I could see her squeeze her eyes shut. Finn glanced at her, then went on.

"Also in Dockyard Marina there is another 25 foot Stingray; in every regard the same as Rick Marchand's, except this boat is named *Hammer Head*, and is owned by Hemming Mathiasen, who goes by the moniker, Hammer, and who lives in New York. The boat is on Dock C, the slip number is 11. This "Hammer" is a very different type of man to Marchand. He has a long criminal history. His money has been gained by a combination of thievery and thuggery.

"Both men are of similar build, with dark hair. Marchand was part of a large fraternity of recreational divers who regularly searched the local waters for clues to 1715 Fleet treasure. Hammer is a guy who knows nothing about boats or diving, or treasure for that matter. For him, the boat is a way of trying to show the world he has worth. It also happens to be where he lives when he comes to Florida.

"On the evening of Marchand's murder, we know, of course, that *Made My Bed* was in her slip and Marchand was on board. The *Hammer Head*, however, was gone. That has been confirmed by the dockmaster, Moema Nuallain."

"And Hammer was on board his boat?" It struck me we needed clarification of the fact.

"His captain told Ms. Nuallain he was taking his boss and some friends for a day of fishing. She saw them pull away at around ten. Hammer was on deck waving a bottle of champagne.

"Now," Finn continued, "we come to Irina, your daughter." He looked sadly at Viviana and Russ.

Viviana began to sob. RJ, who had been sitting passively, exploded to his feet. "What does my sister have to do with this?"

Finn gave him a hard stare, which he then transferred back to Russ and Viviana. "Everything. It's the reason an innocent man was killed."

47

"What are you talking about?" RJ's fists were clenched. He was a bull shark preparing to bump and decide if he should bite.

He was no match for Finn, though, who went completely still. In a chill voice, so low that RJ had to strain to hear it, he merely said, "Sit down, RJ." Almost immediately RJ's ire deflated and he fell back into the chair.

"To continue," Finn said, "about 20 months ago Irina was working at a pawn shop where she handled data entry. Rarely did she work with the customers, but this one day she was asked to fill in for just a few minutes. In that short period of time, Hemming Mathiasen – Hammer – walked in with a gold doubloon.

"Though she carries the characteristics of Down syndrome – the almond-shaped eyes, slightly flattened button nose, the flat profile - Irina is still an attractive and lively young woman. She was captivated by the gold coin and Hammer pounced on this, exploiting her innocence, and persuaded her to meet him later.

"He plied her with alcohol, which she wasn't used to, then he raped her. Nine months later, she gave birth to a child. She is now in a home that cares for the functionally and mentally disabled, many of whom are HIV positive."

"How the hell do you know all this?" It was Russ who interrupted this time. He was breaking out of his torpor, but his eyes were too bright, his color inflamed.

"The police report you filed, naming Mathiasen as aggressor."

"That's privileged information. You had no right..."

Finn flared. "An innocent man has been brutally and senselessly killed. Phill was nearly killed..."

"She was never..."

"Shut up, Viv." Russ snapped at his wife then rose and faced Finn. "Whatever you're implying, you have no proof."

"You think Batista won't find that report? You think he's not already putting two and two together? He saw the diver who shot at Phill; a big, broad-shouldered man." At this, Finn looked pointedly at RJ.

Fear flashed across Russ's face. "RJ had nothing to do with it. I did it. I killed that man."

Total silence gripped the room into which Finn's voice was heard, softly, gently. "No you didn't, Russ." He paused for a long moment. "It was Viviana. Oh, she didn't pull the trigger; she did arrange the hit, though." He turned to her, "Didn't you?"

In slow motion Viviana nodded.

"Viv!" Her husband's face was a mask of misery.

"It's alright, sweetheart." She looked up at him and took his hand. "I'm almost glad it's over." Then she addressed Finn. "How did you know it was me?"

"The flowers were the first thing that clued me in."

She looked confused.

"The huge floral arrangement you sent when Phill was in the hospital. It was overkill. Russ wouldn't even think to send flowers so it had to be your idea. And you hardly know Phill; why spend so much money on a casual acquaintance unless out of guilt?

"It was also the doubloon. I had a friend trace it. He found a dealer who purchased it from a walk-in, no questions asked. The coin was then re-sold to a guy the dealer knew to be Colombian. Viviana, you've hinted that your family in Colombia are somewhat morally reprehensible. I'm betting you would know how to find someone to do your dirty work."

Viviana let out a soft sigh. "Irina simply didn't understand. Mathiasen actually told her the rape was an act of love. Do you believe it? He told her that's how men expressed their love.

"He took her out on the boat after that, with three other men. They took turns in 'using' her. The next morning, before it was light, they put her in the outboard and dumped her on the beach in Fort Lauderdale. Then they hightailed it back to the boat. She was found wandering and mumbling incoherently; bloody between her legs from the rough sex. She had no identification and it was another day before we were able to track her down and bring her home."

By now, I was feeling totally sickened. I was almost ready to put a bullet in Mathiasen's head myself, but the story wasn't over.

"Irina was unable to accurately describe the men who took her, or the boat they were on. And she was so emotionally fragile, we didn't want to push her. Worse still, the bastards left her pregnant and HIV positive."

Sweet Jesus.

"We were advised to abort the baby, but my Catholic upbringing got in the way of that. So once Irina was physically well enough, we brought her home. With the newer treatments available today, transmission of HIV from mother to baby can be less than one percent. We hoped her emotional stability could be improved enough that she could keep and care for her child. She was doing well, and I decided to take her to Palm Beach for a day out together. Irina was at seven months and showing. We were strolling along Worth Avenue when a guy came out of a store. Irina went rigid. He saw her. "Well, well," he said. "If it isn't little Irina." She began breathing in shallow, rapid gasps. It was obvious she was terrified. "Do you want to love me?" she asked.

"Right then I knew. I knew this was the man who had tortured my poor girl. I wanted to rip his throat out but I couldn't move. He laughed…laughed! And walked away, and Irina collapsed. I called for help; people were all around us. A girl came out from the store and I grabbed her and demanded to know, "Who was that man?" She told me: Hemming Mathiasen. And I vowed right then that I was going to kill him."

At that, Viviana seemed to shrink, while Russ and RJ closed ranks around her.

"She nearly lost the baby, you know?" RJ said.

"The child you're now raising," Finn stated and RJ nodded.

"She never did understand the pregnancy. The baby was taken from her without her having a chance to see him. Everyone thought it best."

"How is the baby?" I desperately hoped he was OK.

"Perfect." RJ's smile was tinged with sadness. "His name is Russell 3rd. We call him Rusty."

For a while there was silence.

"What now?" Russ asked.

"Now it's up to Viviana." Finn was firm. "It's time to tell the truth to the police."

"What good would that do?" Russ's tone was pleading. "There's been enough suffering all around."

Viviana pulled her shoulders back. "Finn is right. Because of my hatred and thirst for revenge Rick Marchand is dead. I will never forgive myself for that. And I will always regret that Mathiasen is still alive."

Hours later, Finn and I left the police station after giving our statements. Russ and RJ had continued to argue against Viviana turning herself in and had pleaded with Finn to let it go, but Viviana was resolute and called Detective Batista.

"What will happen now?"

"As best I know, Viviana will be held pending a grand jury. If she pleads guilty there won't be a trial."

I was frustrated. "But she didn't actually kill Marchand."

"She orchestrated everything that happened. What Mathiasen did to her daughter was terrible but the Marchand family deserve your sympathy as well. And Viviana's actions nearly got you killed. I can never forgive that."

Awww. Finn's words made me feel all warm and fuzzy.

"Do you think they'll find the hit man?"

"He's probably already back in Colombia, and I don't see Viviana giving him up anyway."

"And the gold doubloon? Why shove the coin down the corpse's throat?"

"Mathiasen used the coin to lure Irina in. Viviana wanted him to choke on his deed."

It was all dreadfully depressing.

Finn patted me on the back. "Here's something that will cheer you up. I saw your dream detective."

I perked up and raised questioning eyes. I'd been keeping an eye out for him but he was obviously too busy with the Kearns to bother with me.

"He asked if you had anyone special in your life."

"He did?" My heart was doing a little bouncy dance. "What did you say?"

"I told him droves of men were after you."

I slapped Finn on the arm and scowled.

"Don't panic," he grinned. "I said he'd have to go to Timbuktu and back to find a better woman. So he's going to give you a call."

"Yessss!" I threw my arms around him. "You're the best."

TEN

I love that moment when the sun first appears over the horizon, staining the clouds several shades of gold on a backdrop of bright blue sky. The first sounds of awakening were resonating through Mud Bug as I sat on *Time Voyager's* deck, coffee in hand and Shrimp on my lap. The sordid case of the gold doubloon was largely behind us and I was relishing a sense of cleanliness and renewal as the sun's brightness found me. Then I heard my name being called.

"Phill." There was Bert coming down the walkway, waving his tablet over his head.

"There's something you need to see."

"Come aboard, Bert. Coffee's ready."

I scooted Shrimp off my lap and went to get another cup. By the time I came back Bert had opened up the tablet to an article in the New York Post. In addition to being a financial genius and creator of video games, Bert was a speed reader and would zip through several major news sites every morning.

The article headline read: Man Accused of Racketeering and Extortion Found Dead. I began to skim through. "Holy cow!"

"You don't say. Where's Finn? He'll want to know about this."

"I saw them head off for a dawn walk."

At that moment I saw Finn with Moe, coming around the far side of the harbor. Moe was spending a week with us. Well, not exactly with me. Bert had been kind enough to offer Finn the use of the new guesthouse, so I'd had *Time Voyager* to myself – and Shrimp, of course.

I stood and waved wildly. "Hey, you two. Hurry over!"

They picked up their pace and as soon as they were on board I handed the tablet to Finn. "Read!"

He did, while Moe peered over his shoulder.

Police are looking into the death of Hemming Mathiasen, whose body was found floating in the Hudson River in the New York Harbor area. Mr. Mathiasen was well-known to police. Detective Delfina Ronchi stated that Mathiasen had a history of criminal activity, and was currently under investigation for extortion. She declined to say anything further.

Staff at the Porque Bar and Grill told this reporter that Mathiasen was drinking there earlier in the evening with a couple of men. The bartender, who would only give his name as Luis, stated he thought the men might be Colombian. The two men have not come forward since Mathiasen's body was recovered. There is no further information on whether this was a crime or an accident.

"Perhaps Viviana had the last word after all." Moe raised her eyes.

Finn made no comment and I gave him a suspicious eye. "You didn't happen to know anything about this?"

In return he gave a "who me?" look. I was about to start grumbling when Moe broke in. "I think this deserves a new cocktail. Phill, what say you and I get creative and come up with something for this evening?"

"On it," I said. "I'm thinking Licor 43 and cognac. A touch of chocolate bitters might work well with it, too. And let's

call it a Gold Doubloon."

Finn rolled his eyes.

"What? What's wrong with that?" I flung my arms outward in a questioning gesture.

"Gold Doubloon? Couldn't you call it something else? That seems a little tacky."

"Well, it is gold in color."

With a sigh, Finn said, "Alrighty, then."

The end

The next book is:

The Game's a Foot

Become part of the in-crowd and get a FREE short story:

http://lizdodwell.com/signup/

Find all of Liz's books here.

http://lizdodwell.com/books/

Liz Dodwell

Author's Notes

Phew! Another Captain Finn mystery solved. I hope you enjoy reading these stories as much as I enjoy writing them. If you do – well, even if you don't - please consider leaving a review wherever you purchased this book. As an independent author it's not easy to compete out there, and your feedback will help me know what you like.

I'd also love to get to know you on my facebook page: https://www.facebook.com/LizDodwellAuthor. Join me there and tell your thoughts and ideas. I check there every day and answer all questions – honest!

OK, treasure hunters, what about the 1715 Spanish Plate Treasure Fleet, you ask. Well, it was July 30/31, 1715 when a savage hurricane tore the fleet apart off the east coast of Florida as it sailed northward on the way back to Spain. The ships were driven on to jagged reefs where they broke apart like matchsticks, and hundreds perished. The galleons were loaded with precious cargoes of tobacco, spices, jewelry, gold and lots and lots of silver. That's where the Plate Fleet name comes from – plata, Spanish for silver. It was a terrible blow for King Philip V of Spain; nearly bankrupted him. Salvage efforts were begun and more than 5,000,000 pieces of eight were recovered. Then, for nearly 250 years the wrecks were forgotten. Now, modern-day treasure hunters search the sea bed for the fortune that is yet to be found.

Now I need to thank some people, without whose help the Captain Finn series wouldn't exist. First is treasure hunter and friend extraordinaire, Captain Carl Fismer. Not only does he provide inspiration, he makes sure I don't make any glaring mistakes when it comes to shipwrecks and treasure. You should check his site if you want to know more about a real-life treasure hunter and treasure hunting. Find Carl here: http://www.carlfismer.com.

Much gratitude to Dominic Ottaviano, my multi-tasking assistant; to Tracy Nowell, a truly lovely lady and invaluable helper; and my husband, Alex Markovich, as always, for constant support and faith in my abilities.

Lastly, and most importantly, a huge thank-you to you, my readers. Without you, there is nothing.

The Game's a Foot

Time Voyager swayed with the rhythm of the water as we lay at anchor on the Boneyard site in the Gulf of Mexico. On deck, Grace and Michael Bumbry had stripped off their dive gear and settled into a couple of chairs. They were happy, which meant Finn and I were happy.

The Bumbrys were occasional sponsors of our shipwreck treasure hunting expeditions. The quid pro quo for that was a share in potential finds, and the chance to come diving with us. Grace and Michael were active members of NABS, The National Association of Black Scuba Divers and were keen amateur historians of slavery. As such, they had opted for a week at the site where Finn believed we might find evidence of a slave ship.

We hadn't uncovered any major finds, but Michael did turn up a piece of pewter that Finn surmised was the handle of a spoon. That got everyone's adrenalin going because it told us we were likely on the right track. And from Finn's and my point of view, it also meant we could be assured of the Bumbry's continued support.

This was the family's last night. Oh, did I mention Joshua? He's their eleven year-old son; a quiet, serious boy, but smart as they come. He'd earned his Junior Open Waters Divers certification just a couple of months earlier, so had been under with his parents and had collected a whole mess of fossils. The Boneyard site gets its name because the area is replete with fossilized bones, teeth and shells. In his horde Joshua had megalodon teeth, – that's an extinct shark that grew to 60 feet, *Yikes!* – whale ear bones, rib bones and vertebrae. These were all from the Pleistocene epoch, dating back 12,000 to 2,500,000 years ago. And if you think I sound as if I know what I'm talking about, I actually haven't a clue. I'm just passing on the information I got from young Joshua.

So, back to the story. Finn was sort of holding court with treasure tales, though both Grace and Michael were giving him a run for his money. *No wonder Joshua was so quiet, he probably couldn't get a word in edgeways.* Finn was in the midst of describing the procedure a constipated pirate might have to endure back in the 1600 and 1700s. "They'd shoot anything from alcohol to tobacco or even gunpowder up there."

"That must have been pretty explosive," Michael grinned.

In turn his wife quipped, "Thank goodness those remedies have all been flushed down the drain."

Everyone groaned, including Jafet Quintana and Enos Donnell, who regularly crewed with us when we worked the Boneyard. They were all waiting for me to bring out the pre-dinner cocktails – except Joshua, of course. He was busy with his fossils.

I'd come up with a special creation to observe this final evening: a mix of toasted almond liqueur, dark rum, a little almond milk; shaken and served up with a dash of spicy cayenne. In light of the conversation I decided right there and then I was going to name the drink a Clap of Thunder.

"Here we go!" I carried the cocktails out on a tray and handed them around. Grace was now showing Finn the video she'd been taking all week. She had funny clips of us talking pirate-speak, serious clips of how we set up a search grid, and lots of underwater scenes. I left them to it. On board my role was chief cook and bottle washer and I needed to get back in the galley and start prepping dinner.

Joshua was still examining his fossils.

"What are you going to do with them all?" I asked.

"Weeell. I need to finish identifying them all first. Like this one." He held up a large squarish fossil. "I think this might be a whale vertebra. And this one..." about the size of a fat finger, "could be a deer antler."

"How would that get out here?"

"I'm not sure." His frown created parentheses between his eyebrows. "It's a puzzle."

"One I'm sure you'll solve," I said, thinking how he sounded so much older than his years.

He nodded sagely before continuing, "Then I'll take them in to school to show the other kids."

I was about to respond when there was a shriek from the deck. I dashed out, thinking the worst, only to find everyone bunched around Grace with her video-cam. "Phill," she yelled excitedly at me, "we've found it, or at least we've found something. Come see."

I peered over her shoulder at the screen. "Finn says they could be elephant tusks."

It took me a few moments to focus in on what she was pointing at, then I saw it. The outline of four curved objects lying together like spoons in a drawer under a heavy layer of sediment.

"Don't get too excited yet," Finn cautioned. "They could be mammoth tusks, though that's unlikely with the way they're lying. Or it could be a trick of the ocean bed. And we need to figure out where they are first."

I raised questioning eyebrows.

"I don't know exactly where I was when I filmed this," Grace said. "According to the time stamp, it was on day three."

"Well, shi...." *Oops, I was supposed to be watching my language around Joshua.* "Well, surely that's not an insurmountable problem?" I was getting caught up in the excitement. This could be huge.

Someone tugged at my arm. I looked down to see my young friend. His eyes were wide and soundlessly he beckoned with a wave of his fingers for me to follow. At the side of the deck he pointed across the water. "There's something out there, Phill. See? That pink thing?"

I followed the line of his arm with my eyes. There *was* something; a piece of pink flotsam, though it was impossible to say at this distance what it was. My first inclination was to dismiss it, but then I looked at Joshua. "What do you think it is?" he asked. *What the hell.* The grown-ups were having their excitement, why not let Joshua have his. At least for a few minutes.

"The current is bringing it towards us. You go and get the landing net; the telescoping one." He looked at me blankly. "The one that extends." With a brief nod of understanding, he dashed off and was soon back with the net. I let it out to its full 18 feet and we both stood, expectantly, as the object bobbed slowly closer.

Several minutes later I was stretching out trying to snag the flotsam. I still couldn't tell what it was and I just couldn't quite reach it either. If I didn't do something quickly it was going to bob right on by. I snatched some line, tied it round my waist and then to the gunwale rail. Allowing the line to hold some of my weight I was able to gain a few extra inches; enough to tease the object into the net. Then I steadily pulled it in.

It was just a sneaker. A neon pink, child's size air sneaker. Those things will float forever.

"I'm sorry, buddy." I held the net out to him. He didn't look nearly as disappointed as me, but picked the shoe up and studied it intently. *Funny kid. Fossils one minute, yucky sneakers the next.* I turned away to get back to my culinary duties.

"Phill."

I swung back to face him. "Yeah?"

"There's a foot in it."

Liz Dodwell

Liz Dodwell was told so many times that

she really knew how to spin a yarn, she finally decided to put that talent to good use. Taking inspiration from her good friend and real-life treasure hunter, Captain Carl Fismer, she created the Captain Finn Treasure Mystery series.

For several years Liz worked with the Captain, operating his website and arranging talks and treasure exhibitions. "I would dive when I got the chance, but only on a hookah," she says. "I never found anything of real importance, but just knowing I was getting even a microscopic glimpse of history and adventure was truly exciting."

Fueled by an occasional cup of grog, Liz writes from the home she shares with husband Alex and a crew of rescued dogs and cats. For a change of pace she pens stories in cozy mystery and romantic suspense. For relaxation she likes to yodel. (*Just kidding*)

LizDodwell.com

www.ingramcontent.com/pod-product-compliance
Lightning Source LLC
Chambersburg PA
CBHW071208130626
46555CB00004B/1633